The Quest for God

r.d. dickson

Amazon Kindle Direct Publishing, 2021

The Quest for God

About this book: **The Quest for God** is an adventure novel inspired by the personal spiritual experiences of the author.

The Quest for God

Copyright ©2021 Robin Dickson

Cover design and artwork by Patrice Reynolds

Library of Congress Cataloging-in-Publication Data
Dickson, R.D.

The Quest for God /r.d. dickson; ISBN 978-1-7374074-0-9 (eBook); ISBN 978-1-7374074-2-3 (paperback); ISBN 978-1-7374074-1-6 (hardback)
First Edition

Contents

Prologue

Dear reader, I confess I feel compelled to record the essence, as best I can, of my experiences traveling the path to a greater understanding of myself and our Ultimate Creator. We all wonder why we are here—what is the purpose of life? What happens after death? Who and what created life? And numerous other monumental and timeless questions.

These questions dogged me. And I discovered there are answers… Perhaps you will believe these renderings I offer. Or maybe you will chalk them up to an overactive imagination. But, as a wise serpent once told me, if you can imagine something, it exists somewhere in the endless realms of God. Otherwise, you would be creating something outside of God, which is not possible.

Distractions Are Distracting

I heard the call of the wind. There was always the call of the wind. I couldn't remember a time when I didn't hear that drawing sound. Sure, when I was busy doing something and focused on other things, it seemed to fade, but whenever I stopped and strained to listen, the wind was there still. This wind, this sound inside me, always filled me with a restless desire. But I honestly could not put a name or label to the desire.

I lay in my bed covered by night's darkness and closed my eyes to listen, to let the unnamed yearning fill me. On the inner screen of my vision, a small pinprick of white light appeared. I watched without watching and listened without listening. The light grew to enormous proportions and filled my entire field of vision. The wind sound roared, carrying me into the light, into a yellow landscape of rocks and sand.

I scanned my new setting—I was in an outcropping of weathered sandstone—and saw a man with a belted maroon tunic and dark leggings sitting on a huge slab of fallen rock.

Two things stood out about the man: his intense dark eyes in his tanned face, and the brimmed hat. That hat: battered, old, and

downright ugly, he was rarely without it. It sat atop the chin-length black hair of the powerfully built man.

"Shamus" I cried out with delight to see the spiritual traveler. He grinned at me and his eyes sparkled with innate happiness. He had been visiting me in my dreams for some time to help me advance spiritually.

"Little One," he said—for he always called me that, referring to the diminutive size of my female physical body—

"I see the cosmic wind has brought us together again. You are ready… to journey farther into the God worlds?" he asked while examining me intently.

I smiled shyly, unable to put words to the awakening emotions inside me. His own eyes shined as he said, "Your eyes give away the truth of your heart, Little One. But a quest for God is not an easy undertaking. Each step of your journey to the Great Father will be a test for you, a necessary facing of something inside yourself that blocks your vision of our Creator. You see, God already has you, but do you have God?" Shamus laughed heartily at his play of words.

He leaped down from his stone seat. "Let us get started then, while the wind is willing to carry us along the way!"

Shamus whistled softly and two horses came trotting across the canyon floor toward us.

I mounted the white horse and noticed that I too was wearing white--a pantsuit of soft cloth with short sleeves, flaring folds over the legs, and a belt at my waist with colorful stones. Shamus led the way as we rode our horses out of the relative shelter of the canyon onto a great expanse of sand and toward a yellow horizon with twin suns and seven moons. The wind, the ever-present wind, was at our backs.

We traveled into the light of the multiple suns for hours before I spotted a change in the horizon that indicated rocks ahead and something other than sandy flatness. As we approached the changing landscape, I could make out a rock wall fifty feet high that was not natural. Two stone statues flanked an opening.

Shamus peered at me and asked what I saw. I gazed at the statues. The one on the left was that of a musician with some sort of stringed instrument. The statue on the right was that of a nude man and woman in an embrace, the man's hand on the woman's heart between her breasts. Though his turned face obscured her face, they were intent on each other and in love.

When I described what I was seeing, Shamus smiled. He explained that the statues show the observer the two truest loves of the heart.

"You love music, and you love the idea of deep, romantic love. That is what you are being shown."

"But what do *you* see Shamus?" I asked.

"God, my child, I see the face, the love of God."

We nudged the horses and crossed the opening between the statues and rock walls. I looked upon a world of incredible beauty. Gone was the parched and dry sand, the yellow sameness, the twin suns, and seven moons. This was a lush, forested paradise filled with brilliant colors and life. The sound of the wind changed to the sonorous sound of a flowing stream and the twittering and calling of birds winging from tree to tree across the backdrop of an azure sky. Flowers of all colors were everywhere, and the air was crowded with their floral potpourri. I was enchanted. I wanted nothing more than to sit in the shade by the stream and drink in the beauty of this God world.

We dismounted and Shamus took the reins of both horses in his brown hands. Turning to study me, he said,

"You must journey into this land yourself, Little One, for only you can face you. I will wait for you on the other side. If you can cross this land, you will gain something you greatly need in your quest for God. The laws of the spiritual travelers forbid me to give you any more help than these words: 'In the darkest dark of night, the moth sees only the candle flame.'"

He turned and led the horses back through the statue-flanked opening.

I shook my head and thought, these spiritual travelers and their riddled way of thinking, their veiled use of words. What is wrong with just telling me what I need to do? I re-faced the paradise before me and took note that there wasn't a single moth, candle, or black night anywhere in sight.

I put my sandaled feet onto the flat-stoned path that led to the water's edge. I knew I wasn't in my physical body because I felt no thirst, or hunger for that matter when I viewed the water rolling over the rounded stones in the stream. I sat down on the warm grasses of the bank sloping down to the water's edge, watching, and listening.

Hours slipped by, maybe even days—it was hard to gauge the passage of time as this world bypassed the rising and setting of a sun in favor of perpetual sunshine.

Looking around reminded me that the stone path behind led deeper into the forest. I followed the path's beckoning between the trees. This walk in the woods was more beautiful than any trail I ever traveled in my earth world. The trees were all very tall and straight. and at their feet flowers of all kinds saturated with color carpeted the ground. I remembered that the travelers always told me that the God worlds beyond the physical were each increasingly filled with more light and more beauty as one came closer and closer to God.

After walking a while, the stone path ended as I entered a large treeless, meadow-like area. Along the ground, as far as my eye could see, in all directions away from the forest, were trunks, boxes, and door-like apertures on the ground. The trunks were large, small, ornate, simple, wood, stone, beautiful, plain, and so on. I pulled on the hasp of a nearby antique wood-carved trunk to lift the lid and found an array of beautiful silk scarves—the most colorful and wonderfully designed scarves I had ever seen. The next trunk had river rocks, perfectly shaped, and polished by water—all sizes and colors. A large trunk held a variety of clocks…another had jeweled rings, and the boxes were musical and played melodic songs. These were all the things I enjoyed most, things I liked to collect, I thought. How could this be, a field just for me? Well, God can do anything, I mused to myself.

How was I going to decide what to keep, and how could I carry my treasures across the land to meet with Shamus? I had no bag or pack with me. I began fashioning a bag with some of the scarves and lush fabrics I found in the trunks so I could carry my chosen things. With each delightful treasure box, I pored over the contents, again and again, to decide what to keep for myself.

I decided to try one of the numerous doors lying flat against the ground. I pulled on the decorative gold knob of one door and peered inside. I was suddenly at the summit of a summer mountain. Groves of pine trees—I could smell their piney scent—grew to my left. Ahead the summit began its grassy descent to the valley floor. To my right, I saw only a blue sky dotted with cottony clouds. Eagles flew against those white billows and called a warning that scattered all small furry creatures. The eagles circled lazily on mountain pass updrafts. I breathed the crisp, cool air deeply into my lungs. I could stay here a while, I thought to myself. So, I did.

I discovered that each of the doors on the ground, when opened, would take me to a beautiful or adventurous location, such as a Caribbean-type beach littered with perfect seashells and pearls the size of my thumbnail, a fall day in a forest lazily releasing its brightly painted leaves, a never-ending concert of moving music, or the rooftop of a house on a summer's eve with perfect stargazing.
One door allowed me to become like a bird and soar over an ever-changing land—mountains with snow, golden oceans, tropical rainforests—whatever I desired. The ability to fly was so intoxicating that I visited this realm half a dozen times, or perhaps a dozen times, maybe more.

And yet other doorways were portals to places that had no corollary on earth and no words to describe them… When I wanted a change of scenery, I would go back through the door to my field of wonder. I'm sure days, maybe weeks passed, as I explored the trunks, boxes, and doors of my meadow, and gathered the most treasured items around me.

Finally, I stopped my searching on the ground, looked up, and noted that I had come so far that I no longer saw any forest—all was meadowland filled with trunks, boxes, and doors on the ground from horizon to horizon. I also noticed that I had numerous bags of precious items to move along with me. I realized that I had been caught up in the adventure of looking in each trunk and doorway--for the next one, truly, held some other-worldly treasure more beautiful than the last.

Was Shamus still waiting for me, I thought? How could I have let him down? What did he tell me before he left? I could hardly recall his words, for it seemed a long time ago that he gave me some sort of riddle to solve. I gazed at the sameness of the potential treasures on the ground and, for the first time, became afraid because I could not see the way out of this land, the way to Shamus. I sat down on a handy flat-topped trunk to try to remember. Shamus said if I crossed this land, I would gain something I would need in my quest for God. He said I would have to face myself. Yes, I was recalling his words now: "In the darkest dark of night, the moth sees only the candle flame."

"But there is no darkness in this world of endless sunlight," I cried out in frustration to myself.

I returned to examining the meaning of Shamus's statement. Finally, it came to me that maybe he was referring to focus. After all, I had been spending days focusing on all the goods on the ground. But to get out of this land, and certainly to find God, I would have to forget all the baubles, boxes, and treasures and focus on one candle, one light: God. Distractions! That was the lesson of this leg of my journey, I now knew! Finding God requires the single-minded desire of the heart that allows Soul to see the face of God in the Statues of the Heart that guard this land!

I breathed deeply, closing my eyes. That's when it dawned on me that there was no wind here in this meadow. There was no sound. Fighting my rising panic, I forced myself to listen for the sound of the wind. It's always with me, I reminded myself. Listen. Just relax and listen. I thought I heard a small, keening, wind-like sound. Yes! That's it! I put all of my attention on this sound. I let the sound build in me until I could hear it very clearly with my inner ears. My heart began to fill with that restless desire that I now understood as the desire for God. God was speaking to me in the wind sound!

This sound bathed me, strengthened me, and lifted me to my feet. With my eyes closed against all the potential treasures of the ground, I walked onward, focusing only on the sound within me. One foot in front of the other, I told myself, as I followed an erratic path, hopefully to freedom. Let the sound guide me out of this land…I don't need silks, precious jewels—material things--or more adventures to beautiful places—I've had lifetimes of these in the short time I've been in this paradise, I thought, as I walked. Those things blocked my hearing of the wind, the calling sound of God, and snuffed out the yearning for God in my heart.

"God, please take me home," I pleaded.

I must be like a moth to a flame, a hound on the scent of heaven, a flower whose only impulse is to grow toward the warm sun…a…I was stopped short in my soliloquy when I felt a touch on my arm.

I opened my eyes and saw the beautiful face of Shamus the spiritual traveler. I had crossed the meadowland and was back in the yellow world of twin suns and seven moons! Shamus's broad smile was welcoming, but his eyes held both pleasure and pain as he said to me,

"Little One, you have regained the first quality you will need for your God quest."

He reached out, and with great tenderness, stroked his fingers lightly over my cheek.

"Your journey has been long and arduous. You must rest before going on."

He studied me, then answered my unspoken question:

"Child of my heart, you have been in the Land of Desires the equivalent of 12 years."

With this realization, I looked at my beloved spiritual traveler and tears slipped down both my cheeks and onto the pillow of my bed, awakening me to the morning light back in my current life on the physical world time track.

Chasing Shadows

The darkness of this place was stifling. Terror pressed down on me and I felt like my lungs could not inhale. My eyes burned from trying to make sense out of the greyscale landscape before me. Exhausted and beaten, I huddled in the alley between buildings and wondered, how did I come to this place?

Two weeks previously...

Time had passed since my last foray into the God worlds with Shamus, the Spiritual traveler. My days were filled with the routine of rising, work, chores, and resting for a new day. Because of my lesson in the Land of Desires, each night I lay in bed and listened to the wind sound and watched for the light in my inner vision. God's love filled me until I drifted into sleep, however, my sleep was unmarked by nighttime travels, at least as far as I could recall.

One day I discovered a music CD in my mailbox—a gift from one of my friends aware of my love of music. After the evening errands, I situated myself in my favorite easy chair next to the bookcases in my library room to listen to the new music. From the first song, I was completely captivated by this new-age music. It was as if this music and the power to lift me in spirit, thought, and mood. Voices sang in an unknown language with such loveliness that I almost wept from the ecstasy their sound induced in me. I closed my eyes and let the beauty of the sound vibrate through me.

My inner vision filled with warm yellow light and then I was standing on a stone floor at the summit of a low hill. Surrounding the stone circle on the ground, spaced evenly apart, were upright rocks nine feet high and three feet around—a ring of stone sentinels. The sun was high overhead and when I looked into the stone shadows, I found Shamus, the spiritual traveler.

His smile was bright as he acknowledged me, "Welcome Little One. I see the wind of God is still with you," he said. "It is time for you to continue with your quest for God. For your new journey, you will have a different guide."

Shamus lifted his hand to open his palm toward the opposite rock. I turned and looked, and when my eyes separated the spiritual traveler from the shadows, I saw a man with short dark hair and radiant brown eyes. He wore modern clothing, a shirt of soft blue with navy pants.

"Z!" I called out with happiness at seeing my familiar spiritual mentor. It was Z who took me into my first God world: he had chosen me to be his student. And it was Z who had introduced me to other spiritual travelers, including Shamus.

I had been reading years ago about people who had spiritual teachers, so I threw out to the Universe, "Why can't I have a spiritual teacher?"

Shortly after, I had my first meeting with Z in a dream and he explained that when the student is ready, the master appears.

"Hello Shi," Z greeted me with a wide grin. He sometimes addressed me using my true spiritual name rather than my given, American name. When he looked at me, the effect was like mild, warm electricity flowing through me—God's love flows very strongly through this spiritual traveler. He became more serious as he began to prepare me for my spiritual journey. "You will be traveling to a special realm where you will have the opportunity to realize another quality that is needed for your quest for God. You must not fail Shi," Z cautioned, "or you will be caught there for half a breath of God—half an eternity. The laws of the spiritual travelers again forbid me to accompany you in this land, but I will provide help to you if you remember to call on me. If you are ready and choose this experience, step on the blue stone in the center of this circle," he said as he pointed to the appropriate stone, now glowing with an unearthly blue luminescence.

I moved to the indicated stone and when both feet were on its flat surface, I heard Z say, "May the blessings be…" and I was instantly in an unfamiliar land. I blinked my eyes several times to see clearly, but it didn't help. What was wrong with my eyes, I wondered?

Wherever I looked, all was distorted and hazy, without defined shape. This was a monochromatic world comprised only of shades of grey and black. There were thin, long, black, pole-like stretches across my vision with dark blobs at the top. Smaller dark masses moved as if by a slight wind, but I felt no wind. Finally, I saw a black ribbon ahead of me that eventually disappeared into a dark horizon. It occurred to me that perhaps it was nighttime in this God-world, yet there was a lack of detail and a curious two-dimensional quality to everything here. All I could see appeared to be laid out upon the ground. I had the sudden thought that this was a world of shadows only: that which cast each shadow was mysteriously hidden.

I thought about my task—to re-gain something I would need for my search for God—and determined that whatever I was looking for wasn't here. I decided to walk the dark ribbon to my right.

Lifting and putting one foot down, I found solidity and was encouraged that I was on some sort of a roadway. For the next few hours, I stayed between the black edges of this ribbon road encased in darker patches on either side—perhaps some sort of forest. Then I came to a crossing, an intersection of black ribbons. Again, I took the ribbon to the right. Robert Frost's words came into my mind: "I took the road less traveled by…and that has made all the difference."

There were more intersections and even more forks from which to choose. I continued walking, wandering through this shadow forest until I realized that I must be lost. The landscape was still dark shadows decorated by even darker shadows. Seeing only blobs of fuzzy dark things was becoming weary and tiresome to both my eyes and my brain! How long have I been lost, I wondered? I sat down and closed my eyes to rest.

With my eyes closed, I noticed that this was a very quiet God-world. With my inner ears, I heard my constant companion—the wind sound. A blue globe of light stepped into my spiritual eye and I felt the loving presence of Z, the spiritual traveler.

"What do I do now Z, which way do I go?" I asked.

Z's reply came into my awareness and indicated that I was to continue by taking the left fork ahead of me. Walking on, each

time I came to an intersection, I stopped and asked Z the way. After much walking, I finally could see changes ahead. The dark patches became larger and geometrically shaped. This must be a city with buildings, I thought to myself.

In this shadow city, some of the shadows moved. There were long things with appendages, and other moving shadows were oblong. Perhaps these were people and vehicles. Suddenly, I was struck on the shoulder from behind and fell to the ground. I turned my head in time to see a long shadow move toward me and I felt another blow to my body. Other shadows rushed toward me, moving wildly, pummeling me with ferocious hits. I knew that I had to get away or I would be beaten and trapped here by these shadow beings. I raised myself up and quickly crawled between two swinging shadows and then stood up and ran.

Instinctively, I stayed with the darker colored swatches of ground—roadways, hopefully to freedom. I darted between what I thought were two buildings. The darkness of this place was stifling. Terror pressed down on me and I felt like my lungs could not inhale. My eyes burned from trying to make sense of the greyscale landscape before me. Exhausted and beaten, I huddled in the alley between buildings and wondered how did I come to this place? What in me was lacking so much that I would need to be in this shadow world?

Tears stung my eyes when no answers came to me. Shadow beings were milling around the entrance to my hiding place, and I became afraid. Z's words of caution haunted me—I did not want to fail and be stuck in this black and grey world for half an eternity! I moved farther back into my alleyway until I came to its end and could not move anymore. A solidness I could not see blocked my exit and I was trapped.

I cried out to the dark ethers, "Z, help me!"

I crouched down in the alley and hoped that I was as dark as this shadow alley.

That's when Z's voice resonated in my head: "They are afraid of you because they see you are different, not of this world. That's why they are attacking you— the unenlightened often attack what they fear! Your only chance is to become invisible to them."

"But how," I asked, "how do I become invisible?"

"Make a postulate within yourself and then let the Cosmic energy fulfill your postulate," Z indicated telepathically.

I crouched lower and told myself I was invisible! It came to me to blend myself as if atomically, into my surroundings. I imagined that my body was of the same substance as the features of the alley around me. Then I willed it, believed it, and felt it to be so.

A shadow was almost upon me by then. I thought to myself that I would either be invisible, or I wouldn't and turned the whole matter over to God. The shadow being stayed almost on top of me for what seemed God's eternity then moved on to join other shadows. After a bit, they all receded from my hiding place.

Relief flooded me. Though my immediate danger was over, I realized I still didn't know why I was in this world; I didn't have what I came here for! I contemplated the meaning of the existence of a shadow world. Why only shadows and no "real" things? The people of this world know only the shadows, I thought, and nothing of what causes the shadows. How limiting that must be, I pondered. I understood the same limited vision in me, as a human being trying to use human senses to see God. I won't find God Itself using my physical senses, yet I can find evidence of God, shadows of God, everywhere with my human sight and human hearing.

I saw now that my twin desires of the heart--music and love between a man and a woman--are lower world echoes of God's voice, and God's love for Its creation, respectively. I had to ask myself, why seek the shadow instead of what casts the shadow? Discrimination! That must be the second quality I will need in my search for God—to be able to separate echoes of God, that which is *from* God, from that which *is* God. Yet this did not mean that God's "echoes," like romantic love and music, are worthless, but should be appreciated for what they are: gifts from

God for our journeying. I can love, cherish, be grateful for the "echoes" of God in my life, but the key is to not let these be my primary goal.

The realization of God Itself is the only worthy goal in life.

With this last thought reverberating through my head, I was suddenly back in my easy chair at home, and very glad to hear the beautiful music from my speakers and to see the colors and depth of dimension of my earthly room.

Snake Wisdom

The day dawned with fingers of light sneaking through the slats of the blinds in my bedroom. I tugged myself out of bed and toward a hot shower. I noted very real bruises on my body from my close encounters with the shadow people in the Valley of Shadows. Shadowy or not, the beings were quite able to give me a licking! I nursed my sore muscles with the hot artificial waterfall of a shower, happy and grateful for this particular reflection, or "echo" of God—so much gratitude for the invention of hot water!

Days went by as I applied myself to my job and the rhythm of daily living, while at the same time, I was renewed in my desire to seek the Divine. My takeaway from the world of the shadow beings was that there is another trap in our search for God: Getting caught up in shadows of Truth instead of seeking that which casts the shadow. God.

My mental wrangling on the matter came to fruition with a particular dream experience. I became aware, in my dreaming, and found myself in a rock-walled, underground, dank-smelling pit of snakes... Yikes! Hundreds of snakes, staring and throwing out their tongues to vomeronasal sample the new entrant to their lair: me!

One of the snakes slithered to face me, raising its head to my eye level as I sat as still as possible with my back against the cold stone wall of the pit.

"Welcome to my realm" he hissed. "I sssee you are a ssseeker, on a quessst for God."

I noticed the snake had an odd diction with s sounds being exaggerated, drawn-out, and well, hissy.

"I have sssome insssight on the sssubject, though you might not want to accsssept the wisssdom and philosssophy of a sssnake—my kind doesssn't have a very good reputation with your kind. Would you like it better if I were a teddy bear?"

Quickly the snake's head morphed into a teddy bear head with knapped ears, button eyes, and a sewn smile, though still on a snake's body!

He continued, "Divine SSSpirit will ussse whatever messssenger It willsss to reach you. Won't you remember my wordsss better becaussse of my sssnake form? Wouldn't you tend to think lessss of a messssage from a teddy bear?"

He reverted to his snakehead, cocking it slightly and smiling, fangs evident.

I wondered if I ate something poisonous before bed because this experience was so weird and so far outside my comfort zone...

"You ssstruggle with my appearancsse. Your logical mind sssays a sssnake can't talk, can't sssmile, yet thisss isss exactly what you are experiencssing. Why do you not trussst your impressionsssss, your own experiencssing of reality?"

"Mankind is forever reaching for reality, for Truth. In truth, man routinely rejectsss Truth if it isss outssside the everyday physssical experiencsse he callsss life. He dismisssesss dreamsss, out of the body experiencssess, déjà vu, imagination, yesss, and talking sssnakesss, asss formsss of reality. Yet thesse are asss real asss the act of taking out the garbage. Experiencsse isss experiencsse to the ever hungry, thirsssty SSSoul. If you experiencsse anything, are aware of sssomething, that sssomething exissstss, is real, and isss an assspect of the great Truth."

"Let'sss talk about Truth for a moment. Truth isss Truth, however, our undersssstanding and grasssping of it changesss depending on our ssstate of conscioussssnesss. Viewing a tree from atop a mountain a mile away will give you a different experiencsse of a tree than looking at the tree from ten feet away. And it would be a different experiencsse altogether if you are lying under the tree looking up through the leavesss, or sssitting on the highessst branch looking outward… Isss one of thessse visionsss wrong in defining the experiencsse of 'tree' my friend? No, jussst different visionsss, viewsss, depending on where and how you are looking."

"God ability, meaning SSSoul vision, isss able to sssee all viewsss of the tree either at oncsse or by flipping through them--not unlike a child clicking its sssstereograph. Conssscioussssnesss isss like a lensss for looking—it can be a magnifying glassss, a glassss darkly, perhapsss rossse-colored glassssess—in other wordsss it providess parametersss of your viewing. Why have a narrow field of vision when you can sssee panoramically?"

"Why iss thisss relevant?" the snake asked rhetorically. "It isss relevant becaussse you can sssee yourssself asss SSSoul, a Divine being. Or you can sssee yourssself as lowly, human. Or even reptilian. And how you sssssssee yourself will be the lens coloring, no, manifesssting, experiencssess that coincsside with your consciousssnesss."

"If a SSSoul ssseess itssself as unworthy of God, that isss the reality it will manifessst. SSSoul createsss itsss own reality, generally through brainwashing called 'education', whether religiousss or sssecular."

"Now you are wondering if your consciousssnesss matchess that of a sssnake! Hah! But am I not an evolved sssnake? No worriesss, I am taking on thisss form only for you to recall thisss lesssson when you return to your physssical ssself."

"Remember Little One, dream experiencssess are asss real asss any other experiencsse you can have. Now perhapsss you can fashion a way out of thisss pit and the company of me and my fellow sssquamatesss." The snake philosopher sidled away from me.

I looked up at the starry opening above the pit graced by a shaft of moonlight. Closing my eyes, I forced myself to calm and to listen until I heard the sound of the wind inside myself. I then visualized a rope ladder hanging from the top lip of the pit. It only took a heartbeat for the snakes to assemble themselves into a ladder form, heads grasping cell mates' tails and intertwining to make rungs.

My absolute haste to vacate the snake den was my only defense against the nausea-inducing thought that I was grasping and climbing via slimy reptiles. As I reached for the ledge and began pulling myself out of that hellish hole, I heard my snake friend clearly enunciate--

"Go with God. Your next adventure will prove to you that you are Soul."

Then I rather gratefully woke up in my bed, vowing never to watch *Lord of the Rings* again before bedtime.

Journey to the Self

A month ticked by due to an intensification of work at my job. I had put in ten-hour workdays for several weeks when my fatigue and rushing led to an inevitable screw-up on my part. Not the kind to get fired about, but the kind that made me feel bad because, in my mind, I fell short of the mark. I let my team down.

I chastised myself over and over again for my mistake. I just would not let it go. My mental apparatus had its teeth in my consciousness and continually stoked the fire of my feelings of ineptness. Hey, I can beat myself up as much as those shadow beings from the Valley of Shadows! But this bruising was emotional and mental, on the inside rather than the outside.

After a week of poor sleep, my exhaustion peaked. I burrowed into bed and completed a 20-minute contemplation chanting the word HU, a very ancient and powerful mantra. And I began a lucid dream experience. This time, I instantly became aware of being in my room next to my bed. Though full-on night, I could see fine. Standing beside me was Z, my spiritual traveler guide.

"Do you *know* who you are?" he asked.

"I can show you," he said.

I followed his gaze to the slack-jawed, messy-haired lump under the covers on my bed. My feline sleeping companion, Tia, laid on the bed and stared calmly at both of us, while my dog, Jimi Puppy, dozed soundly on his doggy pad.

"That," he said, pointing, at the bulge of my body on the bed, "is your physical body. But it is not *you*."

Then he pointed to me standing next to him. "And that is your astral body, but it is not you."

I held out my arms and looked down at my sparkly, ghost-like body. To my amazement, I was not frightened, just curious. I had traveled to the astral plane many times but never had the opportunity to see both my physical and astral bodies at the same time.

Z relayed to my mind, "Soul is the real you. To gain experience, Soul takes on coverings—bodies if you will—so It can interact on the many planes of God's creation. These planes are divided by consciousness, an aspect of vibration. And on each plane Soul has a corresponding body or covering as a protection from the course vibrations there. The astral plane is closest to the physical plane and is where emotions derive. It is also where most people travel during sleep and what we call dreaming. And it is a heaven: the place where many Souls go when they translate or cast off the physical body at death. But there are many planes above the astral level. Do not be fooled that this is the end of your journey, your quest for God."

I absorbed these words which were conveyed to me telepathically, or by some kind of osmosis or direct perception. The Truth of what Z was saying was so evident I could not contradict it if I wanted to. I *knew* this! I knew these Truths.

Z then waved his hand and the surroundings changed. We were in a library-type room filled with shelves. A large, marble-carved rectangular table stood in the middle of the space. I studied the books, and they appeared strange to me, more like jars. Z retrieved one from a nearby shelf. It instantly became a holographic video clip projected in the air above the jar book.

"We are on the causal plane where the records of past lives are stored," Z communicated to me. "All the lives you have lived on this and the planes below—astral and physical—are archived here. These lives, these many beings are of you, but they are not *you*."

I watched as the hologram from one of my past incarnations came to life. I *knew* I was the male figure in the scene, a powerful Middle Eastern noble who had many wives and concubines. I was with my favorite concubine, but she kept talking, talking, and her chattering was getting on my nerves. So, to shut her up I struck her forcefully in the mouth, splitting her lip. I instantly felt regret for hurting her but could not apologize as that would be a sign of weakness. I also perceived from the holographic clip that she was left permanently scarred by my assault.

Instantly, I *knew* that this was the reason for being born with a cleft lip in my present lifetime. It was karma coming home to roost. I had to experience the effects of my own actions. Karma! The ultimate teaching tool of God in the lower worlds: As I sow, so shall I reap. What goes around comes around… We have many sayings revealing this particular truth, this spiritual law. As a child, I had always wondered why I had been born with this birth defect. And now I had my answer.

And I was filled with shame.

Z softened his words to me: "Shi, do not be disturbed by your past selves. You are Soul, a spark of God. And Soul takes on a human or other lower world body so It can have experiences It could not have otherwise have if residing in the eternal realm, the God Home. And Soul uses a different body lifetime after lifetime for Its spiritual education, perhaps hundreds of thousands if not millions of physical forms, for some Souls want to have every experience possible before returning to the God Home."

"To temporarily reside in a human, astral, or other lower world form is to accept a limited consciousness to have experiences. A lifetime is a great teacher. Soul is on a journey of discovering exactly who It really is, and Its relationship to God, our father, and creator. More than that, reincarnation helps Soul realize Its value as Soul."

"Little One, condemning yourself for action in a past life is like holding a kindergartener at fault because she does not know algebra. Yet, given time and experience with learning the building blocks of lesser maths, the child will master algebra. Such is the journey of Soul in the lower worlds," Z explained.

"You would not knowingly harm another now, in this lifetime. See the difference between the past and present as the yardstick of your spiritual growth. All is as it should be," Z added.

Z waved his hand and the scene changed again. We stood in a greenspace overlooking a modern city with towering edifices flanked by roads and sidewalks in a grid pattern. The buildings sparkled with light, appearing luminescent. Even in the midst of a congested city, flowers and greenery were everywhere with an intensity of color that evoked pleasure. The people of this plane, which I recognized as the Mental Plane, were energetically applying themselves to their tasks. I looked down at my body and it had a bluish tint, as did the permanent inhabitants of this plane.

Z explained that the Mental Plane is the origin of the mind and thought, but that the mental body is not Soul.

It is another covering for Soul so it can interact at this level of vibration and consciousness.

"The Mental Plane is the seat for various philosophies, some religious teachings, mathematics, and modern forms of art and design. But your mind is not you. It is an instrument that Soul uses and which It must ultimately drop before proceeding to the Soul Plane, the first region above the lower worlds of matter, time and space," the Spiritual traveler related to me, again, telepathically.

Z turned to me. "In the physical world, consciousness is thought to be a product of the brain, but that is incorrect. Without Soul animating a physical body, there is no consciousness, no life. This is apparent at death, when Soul permanently withdraws from that body, then there is no consciousness even though there is still a brain in the body. Death is simply Soul moving to another body, such as the Astral or Mental body. When a Soul's spiritual education is complete, It drops all lower bodies and returns to the Soul Plane from whence It started Its quest for God eons ago. I will take you there now. You need to see yourself as Soul if you are to proceed on your quest for God."

Z took my hand, and we crossed a zone so dark and empty the passage of time, and space, was meaningless here. How long we were in the dark expanse was impossible to gauge—it could have been a moment or half an eternity. I could not tell you. There was only the comforting presence of my spiritual teacher to reassure me that this was the way to the next spiritual plane.

A swirling white Light appeared on my field of vision, first small, then growing until we were in the Light, and of the Light Itself. I heard the high keening sound of a flute. The white mist dissipated, and my vision cleared. I saw that all around me were globes of Light. These ovals of Light, Souls, formed an ocean of Light that stretched without end in all directions if directions existed in this world. My body was the same, a globe of Light, as was that of Z. Those around me recognized me and flooded me with vibrations of love and joyousness. Perception was my sense here and I perceived that…that--

I AM AN ATOM IN THE BODY OF GOD!

I AM SOUL.

I AM THAT…

DIVINE.

ETERNAL.

BELOVED.

Other perceptions and knowingness flashed into my conscious awareness. I stretched my senses to the end of all existence and
back again. It was pure revelation: God's plan for Soul, for me…

I understood *everything.*

I also was aware of the dual sensation of absolute ecstasy on the Soul Plane and that my physical body back in bed was crying tears of joy. Then, quick as a wink I was back in my physical body in bed, wide awake and utterly, completely awestruck by my travels in the inner worlds of God within myself.

I immediately realized that there are experiences, truths, and realities for which there are no words, that are beyond the lexicon of human language. Sadly, as soon as I was back in my body, the vast truths I had inhaled ebbed away from me, unable to make the journey into my limited mind and brain. It was like trying to fit the ocean into a thimble.

Lady of the Glen

Shock and awe. I was dazed for three days after my journey in full awareness to the Soul Plane. I had taken in so much Light and energy from higher vibrations that I had the spiritual equivalent of a sunburn. I confess that it was not easy for me to experience the Reality of the Self then return to a humdrum existence requiring the likes of bill-paying, laundry, and meeting the basic needs of a physical body. I was also a little mad at God for showing me so *much* and then sending me back here. Back to such limitations.

The three-day weekend ahead gave me a chance to reassemble myself and process all that I could recall from my inner travel. I decided to take a drive with no particular destination in mind. I packed an overnight bag, just in case, and some granola bars, water, and dog chow, and I hit the road early Saturday morning, with Jimi Puppy wildly ecstatic at the opportunity for a road trip.

It was strangely liberating to randomly select roads, to journey without an endpoint. Hours elapsed as I sang along with Carrie Newcomer, blue-toothed from my phone's memory chip. My thoughts were wondrous clouds scudding across the sky of my mindscreen. It is a very freeing thing to be divested of the association of myself as a human female living in such and such state, working, pigeon-holed by things like my race, age, income level… No longer did I think of this body as being "me." I knew without a doubt that I *am* Soul. Soul who just happens to be using this physical body to get around this physical world. I reflected that perhaps most people have a vague concept of *having a Soul.* But *being Soul* is a whole different thing altogether, a monumental shift in perception, attitude, and starting point.

I drove on, and by late afternoon I entered a verdant valley cut between hulking hills, the lay of the land

disguised by nature's living bounty. As I drove
alongside a meandering brook flanked by towering
maples, ash, and oaks, their roots covered by thick
ground cover, I noticed that I was alone on this road.
No other cars were coming or going. I did not see any
houses or signs of habitation either. I checked my gas
gauge and still had half a tank of gas. The valley and
its road led me onward. Another half-hour was spent
with my gawking at the remote beauty of this natural
basin. The light through the leaves of the trees created
webbed patterns of multiple shades of green that
shifted with the balmy breezes. Both Jimi Puppy and I
loved the wind from the open windows of the car.

I was brought out of my reverie by the flashing idiot
light on my dashboard and the sudden rough motoring
of my car that seemed to be exhaling visible breath
from under the hood. My car was over-heating!

I pulled to the berm. I checked my phone and, of
course, did not have any service deep in this valley. I
propped up the hood of my car, the universal symbol

for car distress. It looked like a hose blew out and emptied the radiator. After Jimi did his business, we returned to the car to wait. Another 45 minutes passed without any passing cars. No possible pedestrians to help me.

Hey, universe! I need help here, I telepathically threw out to the Divine via a quick prayer request.

I put on a HU recording through my car speakers/phone connection and chanted HU, the holy name of God, along with the thousands on the recording. Before the 20-minute recording was done, a Jeep showed up and parked behind me. A woman got out and glided toward me. Yes, she seemed to truly glide, rather than walk!

The lady had golden hair pulled up, with tendril whisps alongside her face. Her eyes were the electric blue of the water that wells up from glacier crevasses. She wore a calf-length white wrap with a white lacy shawl over her shoulders. Jimi eagerly hung his head over the windowsill, his stub tail wiggling frantically, obviously begging for pets.

"Hello to both of you!" she said, her smile easing any panic I might feel being approached by a stranger in the middle of nowhere with no
one else around for miles, and only a smitten, traitorous mutt to protect me.

She stood a respectable distance from the car and peered at me.

"Car trouble I see. And I bet your cell phone doesn't have service here. If you want, I can drive you and your dog to my house, and you can use my landline to find a mechanic. I live a few miles from here. I would be happy to help in any way I can."

This lady exuded warmth and caring. *Lady of the Glen* popped into my mind, but I questioned, where did *that* come from? I certainly didn't know her, though she did seem vaguely familiar.

I grabbed my bag and Jimi and I followed her to her car.

She had a cabin a mile or so away tucked off the paved road and completely enclosed by the forest. The kind of place you had to know it was there to find it. The front porch sported rocking chairs, of course. Flowers and vines adorned the place. Inside, the open floor plan was graced by a leather couch on a braided rug before a stone fireplace and opposite a modern kitchen with an island and stools in place of a dining table. A staircase reached a loft bedroom girdled by a wood limb railing to prevent sleepwalkers from tumbling to the main floor. The lady of the glen had very good taste, her home decorated with colorful art, comfy throw pillows, and a few natural souvenirs— rocks, feathers, decoupaged leaves gathered from the forest. Jimi Puppy had already found a pad on the floor and was sacked out.

I suddenly felt like I was living in a Hallmark movie: It all seemed so *magical.*

"My name is Simha. You probably would prefer coffee, but I think you might like to try my homemade tea. I make the spice mix myself."

I nodded in agreement and she filled and put a kettle to boil on the stove. As she worked, she informed me that a car shop was located about 10 miles away but that it closes at noon on Saturdays.

"I know the owner. Maybe I can talk him into helping you out. We can try, anyway," she said as she handed me a handmade pottery mug of tea.

Simha placed the call and explained my situation. When she ended the call, she related that George, the mechanic, would be out to look at my car around 1:00 p.m. the next day. He had a family commitment that prevented helping me today.

"You can stay here with me tonight. You and your puppy will be much more comfortable here than in your car, and I would love the company! Besides," she added, "I was waiting for you to arrive. I knew you were coming," she added cryptically.

Simha led me out a back door to a patio area with a pergola roof. The late afternoon sun slanted alternating geometric patterns of shadows and light on the flat stones creased by moss and grass. The air was scented of floral blooms and earthiness. I selected a rocking chair and sat savoring my tea. Simha was right, the cinnamon-chai spice of the tea was perfect. Exactly what I like. She excused herself to prepare us a repast, while my half-drowsing in the splattered light lowered my emotional temperature considerably. This little homestead nestled in the forest was like warping into an alternate reality. An enchanted, dream-like reality.

Simha laid a plate of sliced fruit, fresh vegetables, wedges of sourdough bread, and hummus for dipping on the side table between our chairs and seated herself next to me. When she turned to me, I noticed then the intensity of her eyes, and the misty aura of white light emanating from her.

"I see you have journeyed beyond Sohang, to the Atma Lok, and have heard the call of the flute." Her words, the timber, and the vibration of her voice were both electrifying and deeply calming at the same time.

"To see oneself in the true body, as Atma or Soul, is a sacred gift. But it can be a bit overwhelming. The mind, the mental body, prefers its routines and its catalog of known facts and can be unsettled by anything beyond its ken. This is a nice segue into the topic I was asked to elucidate with you, that of healing."

I continued to sip my tea—how did it never run out? And watched as a doe and this year's fawn grazed their way toward us on the patio. Birds chittered and flitted around the feeding stations, birdbath, and berry bushes of the backyard. For some reason, it did not seem at all odd that this stranger would speak to me of spiritual matters. Or that she was aware of my recent innermost travels.

Simha continued. "A disease or disorder arises out of a karmic condition set in motion by the individual who has violated a spiritual law, either in the current or a past lifetime. Many will resist this Truth, preferring instead to cast themselves as innocent victims of life or an uncaring God. Well, God established the spiritual law of karma to teach Soul how to love and be responsible for Itself, so why would God intervene and prevent a Soul from learning these very lessons? That would delay Soul's spiritual growth. The lower planes are a schoolhouse where Soul receives Its spiritual education. Most need to attend the school of hard knocks to learn to live in harmony with the spiritual laws."

"Healing can occur on any of the planes you visited with your spiritual traveler. Such as healing of the body, healing of the emotions, or the mind. Spiritual healing heals all of these, however.

Any remaining karma is removed because the individual Soul no longer needs that karmic condition for Its spiritual growth."

Simha looked to the yard and raised her hand. I noticed then that the deer were joined by a couple of rabbits, a skunk, three squirrels, and a variety of striped chipmunks, mice, moles, and voles. The animals responded by coming forward, weaving themselves around and between us. I touched the sleek deer pelt. A bird landed on my shoulder and sang in my ear. This was delightful!

Simha continued her discourse, "Healing can be complete, as I said, or it can be partial, relapsing, or healing can be gaining an understanding of the karmic causes of a condition, even though the condition remains."

She reached down and picked up the skunk and it curled up on her lap wrapping its prodigious tail around its body.

"What is necessary for healing?" she asked me directly.

"Well," I said, "if I were ill or in need of healing, I would first accept that this experience has meaning. That my illness is not a random act of unkindness from the Universe. I would ask for help from the Divine Spirit, but not to beg to be relieved of the condition, but instead to ask for understanding of what is happening. What am I to learn from this? And also, what do I need to do to resolve the karma, so I don't have to face it again?"

I paused, then reflected, "I suppose I also need to trust the Divine, especially if I don't get answers or relief right away. There is a way forward even if I don't see it initially. All in God's way and God's time sort of thing."

Simha smiled her agreement with my words, and a cloud passed away from the sun suddenly making the meadow-yard around us all the brighter.

She elaborated, "When anyone calls on the Divine for help, often the healing is in the form of greater realization. Going within will lead to a better way to cope with any vexing problem or condition, but the individual must do his or her part. God does not run a spiritual welfare program. After asking for Divine intercession, the individual must be alert as to what Spirit will bring and be willing to seize whatever opportunity is offered. The help could be a nudge to see a certain doctor or healer or the person may realize a change in diet or habits is in order. No matter the request, the Divine will answer, and in a way that is absolutely right for that Soul. But the individual must have the eyes and ears to see or hear the guidance and then act upon it."

I helped myself to some of the refreshments and finally got up the courage to ask,

"Simha, why are these wild animals so…trusting?"

I scrutinized the snoozing skunk on her lap. Her laughter was soft chimes.

"They are responding to the thought patterns we are giving out: Love. It is said that 'all things will come to thee if thee let love enter the heart', and that includes Souls in animal form too. And this brings up the other topic I was tasked to talk to you about—love."

Simha's countenance flowed waves of love, erasing all doubt about the spiritual stature of this great Soul. She zeroed those ice blue eyes on me. "God is love, and Soul exists because God loves It. Outdated concepts such as the Creator as a vengeful God, or that the goal of the quest for God is to merge with God, need to be dislodged from the mind. GOD IS LOVE, and Soul will come to realize that and more but will never lose Its individuality."

"Since we are children of God, we share the same attributes as our Holy Father: Love. But with Soul's advent into the lower worlds and Its diminished awareness, It has forgotten that It is Soul and that It loves because God loves It. The journey of Soul in the lower worlds is one of re-claiming or re-awakening that which is already within. Soul must re-learn how to give and receive love, Divine love."

"These are just words for you right now but soon you will have an experience that will show you the reality behind the words. For now, follow along with me. If God is love, then we, Soul must become love if we want to experience God, what the mystics call God-realization. For God will not permit anything impure to approach It. The most important quality you must develop in yourself--or actually recover in yourself--is love. If you become love itself, you can then experience God, become God-realized. With that high state of consciousness, you will be given your mission, for Soul then knows that helping other Souls on their quest for God is part of God's grand plan."

Simha eyed me and sighed, "We will end here. I have another appointment and need to leave, but you are welcome to help yourself to the food and hospitality of my home."

She gently lifted the little animal off her lap and deposited him on the ground beside her, then went inside.

I sat absorbing her words. A deep sense of inner peace and connectedness to all life draped around and through me, easing the daze I felt ever since my journey to the inner worlds with Z. I watched the sun arc to the horizon, the sky painted prettily with orange and pink brush strokes. I did not notice when the animals returned to their wild ways but realized it was getting late when Jimi called out from inside the house indicating his need to tend to his business.

We passed the evening together, grateful for this little cabin. And the lady of the glen.

The next morning, I awoke, feeling renewed. My hostess was nowhere to be found, but Simha had left a note for me on the kitchen island.

Little One,
I apologize that my duties have led me elsewhere and I am not able to see you off. If you turn right at the

end of my lane, you will find your car about a mile down the road. George will be there to help you between noon and one o'clock. It was wonderful to see you again! Until next time, I wish you well. Remember this great secret—it is love and love alone that can carry you to God.

> *Go with God,*
> *Simha*

Coin of the Realm

I instinctively knew I would not be able to find that little cabin again, even if I tried. It seemed to me that time and space had opened a portal to a place where I could meet with Simha, Lady of the Glen. A place that was both real and unreal.

Days had passed since I returned home, but the experience in the glen still resonated with me. I continued to contemplate upon what Simha revealed to me, and wondered how to open my heart to love, to become love Itself.

I resumed my spiritual studies and practices—reading my spiritual texts, doing a daily spiritual exercise of chanting HU, and listening for the heavenly Sounds within me. I eagerly watched, and waited, to see what Divine Spirit would bring into my life. I reflected on all the qualities needed for my quest for God—focus, discrimination, embracing the reality of the self as Soul rather than as a physical being, and love.

Fall fell upon us and the wind grew a bit of a bite requiring extra clothing to enjoy the out-of-doors. I had always loved the air when tinged with drying leaves, their full-circle journey now complete, returning their elements to their earthly origin.

Jimi Puppy pulled me by his leash along a lake trail one sunny afternoon. The sky was robin egg blue, a cloudless backdrop for the multicolored leaves still clinging to the trees that adorned the park's lakeside. The dirt trail bucked and winded its way through the overgrowth skirting the water. We passed a father and son fishing without luck from a wooded pier jutting out into a lagoon. Wishing them better fortune, Jimi and I continued our trek, but not until he had his fill of pets. It is a cold heart that doesn't cave to the charms of a Schnauzer!

As we continued, I breathed in the very breath of fall and pondered how to become love. How to open my heart to love? I need help, I thought, guidance, or something. I had not been able to recall any inner travels lately during my sleep time. And my daily life had appeared quite routine, though my job always allowed me to help others. For that I was grateful. Helping others always lifted me inside. The intangible payoff that supplemented the paycheck and grew my satisfaction with a necessary work life. I thanked the Universe for the blessing of being able to do good while supporting myself.

I returned home and completed the usual weekend chores, then tucked myself in bed to watch a little TV. After a while, my vision blurred. I blinked my eyes in an attempt to clear my vision, but a pair of huge, brown eyes appeared superimposed over the opposing wall. They were the eyes of Z, my spiritual guide. My heart speeded up,
beating frantically in my chest as if desiring an escape from its ribbed cage. The pain corroborated what I instinctively knew--I was dying.

My vision changed to a swirling mass of blue and green color, a tunnel of color, and I left my body there on the bed to travel the streaming tunnel of Light. As I flew, my life flashed before me. It was like seeing video clips or vignettes of my current life—and I looked and I saw. I noted that collectively these were simple moments—me helping someone, me thinking of another or putting their needs before mine, times when I was unselfish. It was like looking into the heart to see what kind of a person I am. I was astounded. I guess I never thought of myself as a good person…always focusing on the things I lack instead: I'm not brilliant, rich, famous, powerful, or pretty. Yet here was a golden, shining heart and I instantly understood that selflessness was the coin of the realm. Acts of selflessness.

I exited the tunnel of Light into apparent nothingness. But I did not lose even a moment of conscious awareness. My master telepathically told me that now I was to experience God's love. It was like being in a completely dark room and suddenly switching on a bright light. I was flooded with the most unconditional love anyone could ever imagine. It wouldn't have mattered if I were the worst person on earth, the worst sinner, I would be loved exactly the same. Unconditional love flooded me in waves. I am loved! I realized that I did not have to do or give anything…but I *wanted* to. It was not necessary, but I wanted to give back. I wanted to serve, to love, even if I didn't have to. There was no bent-backed old man with a long white beard. There was only this wave, this living electric-like love energy that communicated complete, absolute acceptance. Pulsing and roaring through me, ionizing all my atoms of being.

And I was aware that I can love because God first loved me. That love is a very real thing, not an emotion or a mental concept. That It lives. It moves. It creates. Eternally without end.

Suddenly I was back in my physical body, gasping and stunned. Once again, I wiped tears of joy from my face with the heart understanding that I am now a different person. All that I say and do, think and feel, dream and desire, going forward is dedicated to my Creator, and an expression of Its love. How could it not be so?

Yes, I was aflame with goodwill and love for all after my direct experience with the unconditional love of God. But knowing and doing are two separate things, I was soon to discover.

I Am That

Certainly, my death-bed experience showed me that death is just dropping the body and stepping into another plane of existence. No more dramatic than going from one room to another in your home.

I mused that I must have needed an actual death-bed experience so that select moments of my life would flash before me allowing me to see what sort of person I am. Most important, the yardstick I had always used to measure myself against and indoctrinated in me by human culture had nothing, nothing at all to do with what God looks for in us, deep in the human heart. This experience laid bare for me that the whole goal of the parade of lifetimes is simply to learn to be selfless. To learn how to *agree* to give and receive unconditional love. Because that's what God Is, and Soul is a spark of God, cut from the same cloth. I had the answer to the question, what does God expect of us, want us to do with our life here—the purpose of life? Now I had more than a mental understanding, I *knew*. Knowledge borne of the kiss of God Itself.

I reflected on how spiritual hunger either consciously or unconsciously drives each Soul. All of our seeking—whether material, emotional, mental, or spiritual —derives from this hidden need to resume our direct experience of God's love. Soul is exiled to the lower worlds, though not orphaned, trying on one body, one overcoat after another until It can regain an improved awareness of Itself as Soul, then of God, Divine Creator. With some degree of sadness, I realized that the only thing standing between me and the love of God is *me*. The words of my spiritual teachers came back to me about the need to face inside myself that which blocks my vision of the Creator.

And while words fall far short of describing the wondrous majesty of divine love and our journey of reclamation, I decided to try to draft a poem about this spiritual progression. It was a release to rebalance myself after the awesomeness of divine, unconditional love. I offer it here to the reader with my humble apology, for I am no poet, and yet was moved to scribe something to hint at what the driving force of life is in the many lifetimes of the physical worlds, God's schoolhouse.

I am a true Voice,
A splinter of Light
Shot into the darkness.
I am everywhere, and am all things—
The mountain of stone,
The Eagle at the Ninth Gate,
And all that is in between.
I play at life to remember,
And the wisdom of the ageless ages
Is mine to bear forth.
Born of the Song of God,
I have my Father's eyes to see,
And ears, to hear His call
To serve all as myself,
For love is my gift to give.
I am Divine, Eternal, Beloved.
I am Soul,
Yes, I am That.

Tests of Love

It was a Tuesday when my phone rang. My father wasn't doing very well. He was squadded to the hospital because he could not get out of bed, fell to the floor while attempting, and couldn't get up even with Mom's help. Just a few months back, Dad had hung a new screen door on the back porch and ran the rototiller in the yard. So, this rather rapid regression in physical ability was new and unexpected.

After three days in the hospital, the doctor shocked me by saying my 80-year-old father needed the care of a skilled nursing facility. So, Dad would be transferred by ambulance to a nursing home. He was bedridden, unable to feed himself, and had trouble speaking. When he did talk, his speech did not make sense. I had lost my father—who he was as a person--and I didn't know why. The doctors called it Alzheimer's…but as a professional clinician, I knew his rapid losses did not fit the pattern of Alzheimer's dementia and that there had to be something else causing Dad's severe motor and cognitive decline.

After a month or so, the onset of fever led to another trip to the hospital. This time, I requested a different hospital in the hopes of getting a cause, prognosis, and/or treatment plan for Dad's neurological symptoms. A thorough geriatric assessment would be completed while he was being treated with intravenous antibiotics for a urinary tract infection.

Mom and I visited Dad in the hospital daily. He talked infrequently, didn't always make sense, and constantly clung to the bed rails as if he would fall in space if he didn't hold onto something. It was emotionally painful to see my father like this as he had always been a vibrant, strong, and happy man.

Dad's roommate at City Hospital was an 82-year-old man who was receiving blood transfusions while the doctors tried to pinpoint the reason for his low blood volume. I knew this because "Norm" was loud and never seemed to stop talking. When anyone came to see him, nurse, or visitor, he would go on and on about topics like edema, endoscopies, arthritis, financial investments, and cash flow problems, politics….and so on. He seemed to thrive on having an audience and when he got to talking, his loudness prevented carrying on our own conversations. Norm's talking was nonstop, and his audience couldn't get a word in at all! Norm was demanding of both his visitors and the hospital staff. Even when he was alone, he would not be quiet—he talked out loud to himself and even answered himself. We knew exactly what he was thinking all the time: he was unhappy with his life because of pain in his knees and hips and difficulty getting around. Norm repeatedly said he just couldn't handle things and did not want to continue living with his perceived poor quality of life.

I sat on the other side of the cloth privacy curtain listening to Norm's talk and wished my Dad had Norm's energy, and intact cognitive and communication abilities. Norm was still Norm and could take medication for his arthritic pain, and if necessary, even use a wheelchair to get around. I became angry at Norm for thinking he had poor quality of life when my Dad was clinging to the bed rail, unable to eat, drink, speak coherently, or get out of bed. I was angry with Norm for his constant talking. His self-centeredness was appalling, and I thought he was the most irritating person I had ever met! Several times during my day-long visits and conferencing with Dad's doctors, I had to leave the room to get away from Norm to gain peace.

At home in bed at night, my mind would return to Norm. Generally, I am a patient, sympathetic and accepting person, but Norm had exceeded even my high acceptance level. It bothered me that I did not like him, that I had such negative thoughts about him. The all too human, angry part of me was warring with the spiritual side that said I should be able to give at least charitable love to all. Here was a real test for me. I was desperate to get rid of this anger, a very destructive emotion.

I had read in a book that one way to deal with someone you don't like, or have a conflict with, is to imagine having a conversation with them, you know, to try to work things out. So, I imagined talking to Norm. When he started his (imaginary) talking about his medical problems, I was sympathetic, saying that I could see that his pain and loss of skills were difficult for him. He went on, in our imagined conversation, to say that he didn't want to keep going this way. I agreed that we all have a choice. In my Soul-to-Soul conversation, I imagined telling him:

"Norm, you can embrace living, or you can embrace dying. But know that when you stand before God, He will look into your heart and see the moments in your life when you were kind and thoughtful to others when you gave without expecting anything in return. This is the true currency of life. Do you want to be poor when you stand before God?"

I then ended my "conversation" with Norm by saying, "the blessings of God are yours Norm."

The next morning, I picked up my Mom for our daily hospital visit to Dad. Norm was still there, awaiting another medical procedure. The same friend who visited Norm the day before came back. Instead of steamrolling the friend with talk of his medical procedures, Norm thanked Ed for visiting him and for doing the errands requested the day before! Norm asked Ed repeatedly if he would like something to drink, some hot chocolate or something, and suggested that Ed call the cafeteria and order lunch—he offered these options to his friend four or five times! Amazing!

Yes, during my remaining visits with my father, Norm was still too talkative, but he seemed brighter, a little happier, and more accepting of his medical problems. He was nicer to his friend and the medical staff that came by, at least during my time in the shared hospital room.

I was surprised, and grateful, for the opportunity to see a more positive side to Norm, and for the dissipation of my anger for him. Who knows, maybe he decided to embrace living after all. It occurred to me too that this was a continuation of my spiritual education about focus and discrimination. I have to catch myself when I slip from the path of love. As long as I have the physical, emotional, and mental coverings of the lower worlds, I will be prone to responding to their nudges. But I, Soul, am that which watches and corrects the course as needed. Soul is what is aware of the grumbling of the belly, the flash of anger at our spouse or the rude driver and notes the myriad mental wisps that meander into criticism and a thousand other negativities when diarrhetic self-talk—thinking—runs free.

Tests of love. Z had told me, many times, that Soul is tested during Its spiritual education, just like in our physical world schooling. I gave myself a C+ in this test due to needing a few days to get myself to a higher, more loving place with Norm.

After all my efforts to hang out in the hospital to ensure being there when the doctors strolled in, they never did tell me what caused my father's symptoms. But Divine Spirit did: I awoke one morning with the word *atherosclerosis* on my lips, and thinking, what the heck is atherosclerosis? When I looked it up online, the symptoms fit Dad's perfectly.

Collapsing the Time Track

I stood in a column of white-gold Light in the inner world valley where major spiritual rites are held and have been held since the start of time in this cycle. Spiritual masters, a multitude of them, accomplished travelers all of the spiritual realms, stood nearby to witness my ceremony. I was reminded of my real name throughout eternity, Beng Shi.

This was my moment of achieving spiritual mastership.

Then it was gone, just a brief snippet of a future who knows how far in advance of where I am today in consciousness and spiritual growth.

Given to show that, yes, one moment somewhere down the time track, I will achieve my life's goal and take up my mission of helping others on their quest, their journey back home to God.

It also showed me that I ain't there yet! How inspiring, and demoralizing, at the same time.

The energy from this brief futuristic visit was like a slap, and I got out of bed fully awake now, breathing deeply. I had been time traveling during sleep! A word, more a Sound, whispered to me: Shangta. the name of this valley amid rocky peaks that dare to transcend to pierce the clouds. I felt like I was enveloped in warm honey, an incredible sense of well-being.

And since sleep seemed as distant a goal as my attaining spiritual mastership, I made a cup of tea, arranged my velvety blanket around me, and settled into my favorite recliner to do some spiritual reading and contemplate on what it would be like to be God-realized. Living a God-directed life. Unlimited in my ability to be compassionate, loving, helping. Unlimited by space and time and able to be anywhere, any far corner of any universe, plane, or realm of the Holy

One. Continuous access to the love and wisdom of God and Its Holy Spirit. Heady stuff.

The gift of God is that each and all of us will one day achieve this high state of consciousness and will return to the God Home, no longer under the weighty thumb of karma. No Soul is left behind. No Soul is ever lost on Its journey—It is just gaining more experiences. Even the most depraved and presently indifferent to the spiritual life will someday achieve spiritual maturity and go home to God, taking up their chosen divine duties in the cosmic order. It matters not to our Creator, or the spiritual helpers of the realms, whether Soul takes a day or a zillion zillion days to achieve spiritual mastership. My impatient heart wished otherwise, but there is no need to hurry along one's journey, the quest for God.

"You've had many important experiences lately," Z intoned to me. He had silently entered my conscious awareness and took a seat across from me. His astral body shimmered, chimera-like, but real, nevertheless.

"What is the key to gathering and maintaining a high state of consciousness of the Supreme One?" the spiritual traveler asked.

The ever-present Socratic teaching method of the spiritual travelers did not escape my notice.

Pieces parts of my learning flitted before me. Things like the need to face inside myself that which blocks my vision of the Creator. Focus and discrimination; seeing oneself as Soul or divine, rather than human; love; surrender. My thoughts stretched along the tools used too—spiritual exercises, inspirational readings, the HU mantra, creative imagination, affirmations, direct experience with the Holy Spirit seen as Light, and heard as Sound, like the wind-sound I had heard from an early age in this body.

A key, a single key? To distill my experiences down to one simple key…seemed impossible.

"I don't know Master," I truthfully replied.

"Let's take a walk." Z and I were instantly on a packed track in some inner world forest. The wind played lightly with the tree's leaves. The plants and trees were all chatting with one another, but not in a human language. It sounded more like a humming resonance. My impression was that they were enjoying the Light from the Creator, as it shone brightly in this world. Life abounded here—plants of all shapes and hues of leaves, flowers of every color, birds winging and warbling, and the wondrous talkative trees.

We traveled without speaking (communicating) until the track changed to a walkway of white pavers flecked with the essence of diamond chips. This led to a clearing dominated by a temple of grand proportions, vaguely Romanesque in design with fluted pillars. Z led me up the marble steps and into this house of imperishable knowledge. I knew that these temples were present on every plane and sub-plane of the God-realm because I had visited some in my dream travels, but this one was new to me.

"This temple is on the Soul plane," Z said to answer my almost spoken question.

"Within this temple is a place for you to come to get answers directly from the Divine Energy, that which the Creator uses to create all life." He further led me down a hallway to the right and through massive double oak doors, their stain deepened by millennia. The room was dark around its perimeter because of a brilliant shaft of white-gold Light in the center highlighting a huge tome atop a marble dais.

"Step into the Light and pose your question. The book will arrange itself to give you your answer—the answer most needed, most appropriate for your current state of consciousness. You see, all Souls continue to grow in consciousness. There is always another step to take. Always. This is a fundamental principle of God's order. What is a perfect guidance for one state of consciousness may not fit another, once Soul has had additional experiences, additional growth, and realizations," the spiritual master explained.

I stepped into the Light and up to the podium. I formulated my question for the ethers: *Of all the many ways I can use to achieve God-realization, which one should I focus on now?* Instantly the book flopped open, pages turning without a guiding hand until the right page was found and the text I needed stood out on the page:

With love, you have all things. Before any action, ask, what would love do? When thinking and feeling, ask, is this borne of love? Turn your face to love and you will turn your face toward God.

The Light swirled around me, penetrating my aura, enabling me to grasp the simple Truth of the awesome power of love. Like a good cleaning, It stripped away that which I no longer needed; that which dimmed my conducting of the Light as It flows through me and into the worlds. I wanted to love. I wanted to turn my face to God.

I gazed at my spiritual guide, and smiled, as love, Divine Love, flowed in, around, and through me without barriers. A sense of wholeness, a recognition actually, consumed me, as I awoke in my recliner, my cold half-cup of tea on the table beside me.

Over the next few days, I penned a poem to reflect that it is love, and love alone, that can restore our wholeness, our reality as Soul. Love, or the memory of it with God, is the driving force of the quest for God. My quest for God.

I am the song of the wind
In the darkest part of night,
Calling you to me,
The shadow of your own beating heart,
Your next breath—
I am your other half.
I am the cool wind which bites
That you might never forget my presence.
In the stillness of yourself,
My essence lingers,
And waits for you to call me forth—
Your other half.
My touch is searing to the heart,

The Quest for God

While gentle to the flesh,
My song, a siren to the ears,
A vision to be faced.
I am the mystery of your secret longing,
And the very key to life,
The smile in your eye,
And the anguish of your aloneness,
I am your other half—
And my name is love.

My experiences have led me to this point. I have a name for the restlessness driving me—a quest for God. I finally spanned the difference between mental knowing, based on thinking, and spiritual *knowing* or realization, based on direct experience. The latter is unquestioned and can never be taken away by another. Or doubted. Truth inhaled uncovers a core of serenity and strength, the bone structure of Soul.

I am fortunate enough to have wonderful God-realized spiritual masters and tools to assist my quest. I *know* that I am Soul, and God-realized too, even if the latter quest in this lifetime has yet to be manifested completely. I am aware that the quest for God is a gradual process, not a lightning bolt phenomenon, that is gentler and less unbalancing for Soul clothed in the human form. I also grasp that my realization of the Divine Power—Divine Love—will continually expand because the Unlimited is without limits.

My frenzy to go home to be with God now replaced with a rich enjoyment of the actual journey toward the goal. A journey where I ponder how to give, how to serve all, with love. A journey where I recognize that all who are in my universe are meant to be there, and treasured, even if challenging to me. Though I might slip in my execution of a love-filled path from time to time, I have the foundational experiences to bootstrap myself back to a higher spiritual plane. All experience is savored as grist for the mill that grinds and polishes me to a lustrous white Light, a Light that orients toward helping others on their quest for God.

The enLightened Soul realizes who and what It truly is and will not be poor before Its Maker. It is inherently aware of the inextricable link between Its own quest for God, for love, and the quests of fellow Souls, and reaches across that gulf to extend a helping hand. Spiritual vision reveals a net of highly evolved Souls cast across the planet, and all the collective worlds of matter, space, and time, each working in harmony to advance the Soul of mankind, one by one.

I joyfully look forward to the many opportunities for giving Divine Love the Universe will gift me with the rest of my days.

I look forward to meeting you, my fellow seeker.

Final Note

Ancient cultures valued dreams for insights, prophecy, and guidance. The modern world has overlooked dreaming because of the challenges of applying scientific principles to researching the phenomenon of dreaming. And due to a fundamental lack of understanding of what dreams are: Soul's travels apart from the body during sleep. Dreams are as real as any other experience. And dreams, and other so-called mystical practices, are valuable sources of spiritual growth for the venturesome Soul.

I hope you are now inspired to advance on your own quest for God. Wondrous spiritual adventures await you dear seeker—whether these occur via dreams, meditation, contemplation, out-of-the-body experiences, or your daily life.

And if you ask, one or more of the Universe's many spiritual helpers will be happy to walk alongside you.

About the Author

Author of compelling short reads long on punch, the writing of r.d. dickson is of a genre best described as *New Age.* Transcending both fantasy and sci-fi, the author offers futuristic and other-worldly characters, plots, and adventures. The author has a Master of Arts degree in Clinical/Counseling Psychology, graduating *summa cum laude*, and resides in Ohio, splitting time between writing and helping individuals with developmental disabilities lead self-empowered lives.